This book belongs to:

....

....

Retold by Gaby Goldsack
Illustrated by Kim Blundell
Language consultant: Betty Root

This edition published by Parragon in 2009

Parragon
Chartist House
15-17 Trim Street
Bath BA1 1HA, UK
www.parragon.com

ISBN 978-1-4075-0654-8

Printed in China

Beauty and the Beast

Bath New York Singapore Hong Kong Cologne Delhi Melbourne

Notes for Parents

These **Gold Stars**® reading books encourage and support children who are learning to read.

Starting to read

• Start by reading the book aloud to your child. Take time to talk about the pictures. They often give clues about the story. The easy-to-read speech bubbles provide an excellent 'joining-in' activity.

• Over time, try to read the same book several times. Gradually, your child will want to read the book aloud with you. It helps to run your finger under the words as you say them.

• Occasionally, stop and encourage your child to continue reading aloud without you. Join in again when your child needs help. This is the next step towards helping your child become an independent reader.

• Finally, your child will be ready to read alone. Listen carefully and give plenty of praise. Remember to make reading an enjoyable experience.

Using your stickers
The fun colour stickers in the centre of the book and fold-out scene board at the back will help your child re-enact parts of the story, again and again.

Remember these four stages:
• Read the story **to** your child.

• Read the story **with** your child.

• Encourage your child to read **to you**.

• Listen to your child read **alone**.

Once upon a time there were three sisters.

They lived with their father in a cottage.

The two older sisters were greedy.

But the younger sister was kind and pretty.

Her name was Beauty.

One day their father had to go to town.

"What would you like for a present?"

he asked his daughters.

"A ring!" said the eldest sister.

"A dress!" said the middle sister.

"A red rose!" said Beauty.

11

The father rode off to town. He bought a ring and he bought a dress. But on the way back it became dark.
"I'm lost!" he said.

At last he found a big house.

There was no one at home.

Inside the house he found food and a bed.

13

In the morning the father went into the garden.
He saw a rose bush. He picked a red rose for
Beauty. Then he heard a roar.

It was an ugly beast.

"I gave you food.
How dare you
steal my rose!"
roared the Beast.

How dare you steal my rose!

"But it's for my daughter!" said the father.
"Then you must give me one of your daughters
or you will die,"
said the Beast.

It's for my daughter!

The father was sad and went home.

He told his daughters what the Beast had said.

"I will go and live with the Beast," said Beauty.

So the father took Beauty to the Beast's house
and left her there. He felt very sad as he rode off.

The Beast was always kind to Beauty.
Beauty liked living with the Beast.
"I like living here but I miss my family,"
she said.

One day the Beast gave Beauty a magic mirror. "When you look into the magic mirror you will see your family," he said.

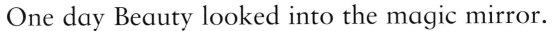

One day Beauty looked into the magic mirror.
She began to cry.
"Why are you
crying?" asked
the Beast.

"I can see my father," said Beauty.

"He is ill. I must go to him."

"Go!" said the Beast. "But you must come back to me or I will die!"

My father is ill.

Beauty went home.

She stayed with her father and he got better.

But she did not go back to the Beast.

One day Beauty looked in the magic mirror.

She saw the Beast. He looked very ill.

"I have broken my promise," said Beauty.

"I must go to him!"

I must go to him!

Beauty found the Beast lying under his rose bush. "Please do not die," she cried. "I love you."

As she spoke, the Beast turned into
a handsome prince.
"You have broken the spell!"
said the Prince.

The handsome prince told Beauty that a witch had turned him into the Beast. Beauty had broken the spell by saying "I love you."
Later Beauty and the Prince married.
And they lived happily ever after.

Read and Say

How many of these words can you say?

The pictures will help you. Look back in your book

and see if you can find the words in the story.

father

Beauty

Beast

Prince

sisters

dress

cottage

ring

rose

mirror

29